Helen M. Todd

NO ANIMAL IS PERFECT

AUSTIN MACAULEY PUBLISHERS™

LONDON • CAMBRIDGE • NEW YORK • SHARJAH

A CIP catalogue record for this title is available from the British Library.

ISBN 9781398431737 (Paperback)
ISBN 9781398431744 (ePub e-book)

www.austinmacauley.com

First Published 2022
Austin Macauley Publishers Ltd
1 Canada Square
Canary Wharf
London
E14 5AA

DEDICATION

To Alexandra and Isabella with love from Nanny xxx

ACKNOWLEDGEMENTS

For Mike – thank you for your support and encouragement.

James the wise old jaguar walked
through the forest floor,

And as he did, he realised he was different;
and what's more,

No animal is perfect -
in fact, some are so unique,

He lay in the forest undergrowth
and took a little peek.

Mia the squirrel monkey
causes mischief every day

She likes to sneak up on her friends
and then she runs away.

She gets the squirrel monkeys to count up to ten,

And when they are not looking,
she sneaks up on them again!

Adam the armadillo has a very scaly neck.

He is different from the others
as his skin pattern is check.

He joins in with his friends as best as he can.

They shout, "You are different."
He replies, "Yes I am!"

Ralph the colourful toucan has a very shiny beak;
Although he is very proud of it, he sadly cannot speak.
Whenever his sister sings her favourite song,
He wishes he could join in with her and sing along!

Jack and Jill the lemurs try to be fast on their feet;
They only stop for fruit for lunch, as they do not eat meat.
They are glad they have each other,
and mum and dad makes four.
They play around together on the forest floor.

James the wise old jaguar walked on some more,
And as he did he looked around the busy forest floor.
No animal is perfect, he thought, falling to his knees,
And watched the animals round him
as he hid amongst the trees.

14

Bella the orang-utan swings through the trees;

She sometimes finds it difficult
as she just has one knee!

She likes to be just like her friends -
they can run, jump and fly.

Whenever Bella can't keep up,
she watches them rush by.

James the wise old jaguar walked on some more,
And as he did he looked around the busy forest floor.
No animal is perfect - in fact, some are dangerous!
He was careful where he walked
about in case he got hurt.

Jake the anaconda is a very dangerous snake.
He scares the animals easily - watch out, he will take
A bite when they're not looking, or he'll really make them run.
He loves to cause commotion, he thinks it is great fun!

Yvonne the tarantula has long and hairy legs.
She likes to catch the insects and loves to hear them beg.
But the insects know her secret: they count up to three,
Then they tickle her all over and set their friends all free!

Lucy the poison dart frog plays in the sun.

Nobody can stop her, as...
she can't hear anyone.

Her friends all laugh, and shout,
and cry and play peek-a-boo!

When they sign things to her
she loves to join in too.

Kevin the King Vulture really does think he is King,
He looks out for his dinner as he spreads his giant wings.
Nobody seems to like him; but he tries his very best
Not to look so scary as he looks out from his nest.

James the wise old jaguar walked on some more,

And as he did he looked around
the busy forest floor.

No animal is perfect, he thought
as he gave a little smile

He watched animals play around
for a little while.

William the ocelot has a birthmark on his face,
He hunts for prey so quietly as he roams about the place.
The animals think he is scary so they run away.
They will come across the ocelot on another day!

Leo the crocodile swims down the stream,
He likes the animals in the water to think he isn't mean.
And when the fish swim past him
his mouth gently opens wide,
If they are not too careful they will end up inside.

Samuel the smiling sloth has many places to go,

He tries to keep up with his friends
but he is really really slow.

To show he could be sporty he tried to win a race,

But the animals ran past him
as he couldn't keep their pace!

Terrence the tapir loves to get wet with his dad,

He can't swim like the other tapirs
and this really makes him sad.

Dad says he will give him lessons
but it hasn't happened yet,

So he splashes in the water,
getting everybody wet.

James the wise old jaguar walked through the forest floor,
And as he did he realised he was different,
and what's more.
'No animal is perfect, and that's how it should be,
Yes, no animal is perfect and that includes me.'

The message in this story is that
we all have different ways.

We might not be the same as you
and this is fine, okay?

We might be tall, we might be short,
we might have different skin;

We might be slow, or perhaps can't hear,
or have dimples on our chin.

So have a look around you: isn't this so true?

None of us are exactly the same,
and that's what makes you, you!

The jaguar smiled wisely as he gently shook his head.

"Goodnight dear friends,"
he called out as he settled in his bed!

ABOUT THE AUTHOR

When Helen's children were little she loved to write stories and read them just for fun. Now her children are all grown up and she has grandchildren, she has decided it's time to start writing stories for other children to enjoy.

Helen lives in Bedfordshire with her husband and her cat. Her children and grandchildren live close by.